SECURITY

D0807697

This book
belongs to _____

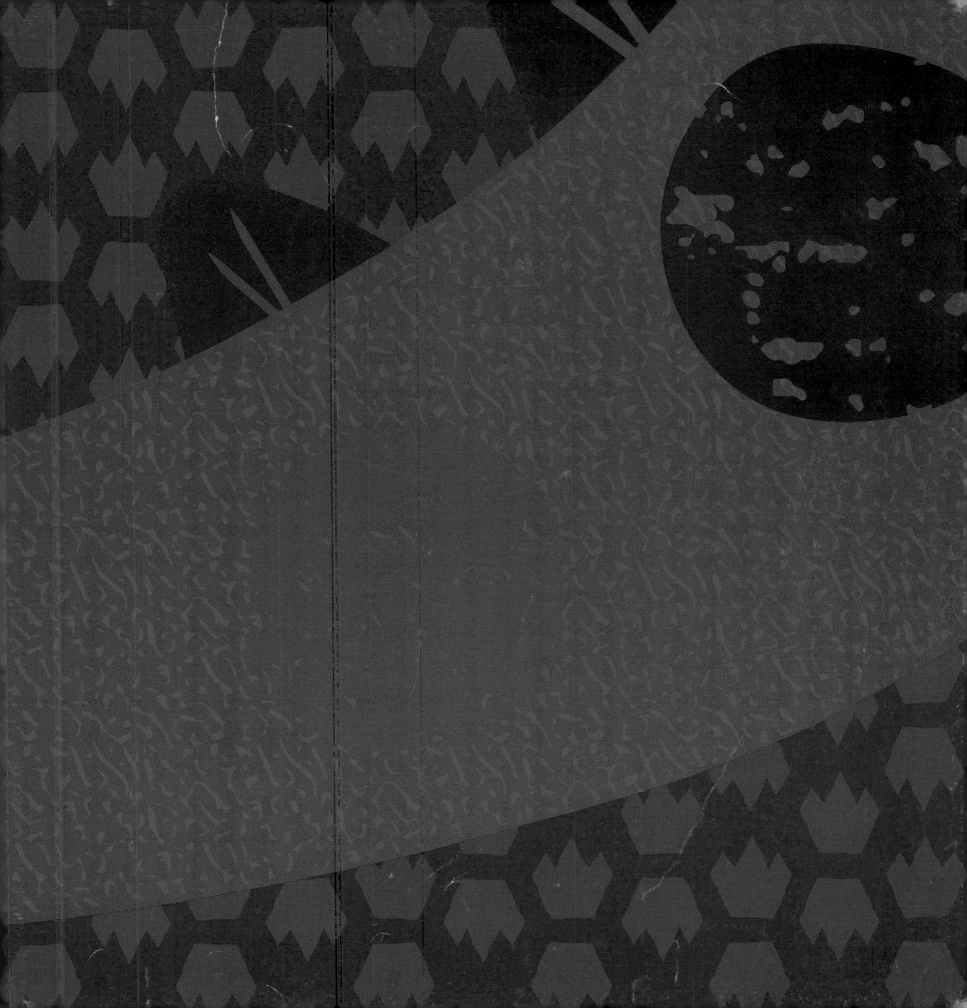

Written by Rosie Greening.
Illustrated by Stuart Lynch.

NEVER touch A
T. rex

SECURITY

T. rex Team
Raptor

Rosie Greening • Stuart Lynch

make
believe
ideas

WELL YOU CAN'T.

SECURITY

Rules

Here's the rule:

① You must never touch a T. rex, unless you . . .

. . . point to your nose.

There's no way you can point to your nose. Just you try!

How did you do that?

Okay, this is the **real** rule.
You must **never** touch a  T. rex,
unless you . . .

. . . POINT to your nose

and TOUCH your toes!

Ha! Try those if you
think you're so clever.

Okay, **genius.**

The **actual** rule is this:

Never touch a T. rex,

unless you . . .

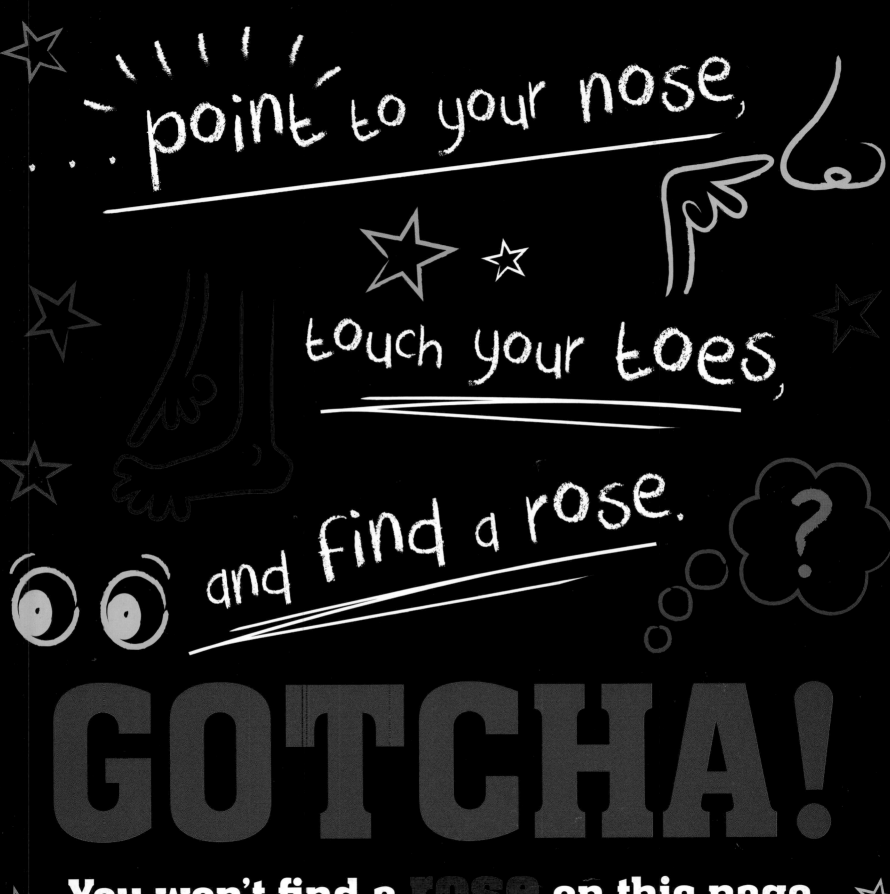

point to your nose,

touch your toes,

and find a rose.

GOTCHA!

You won't find a **rose** on this page.

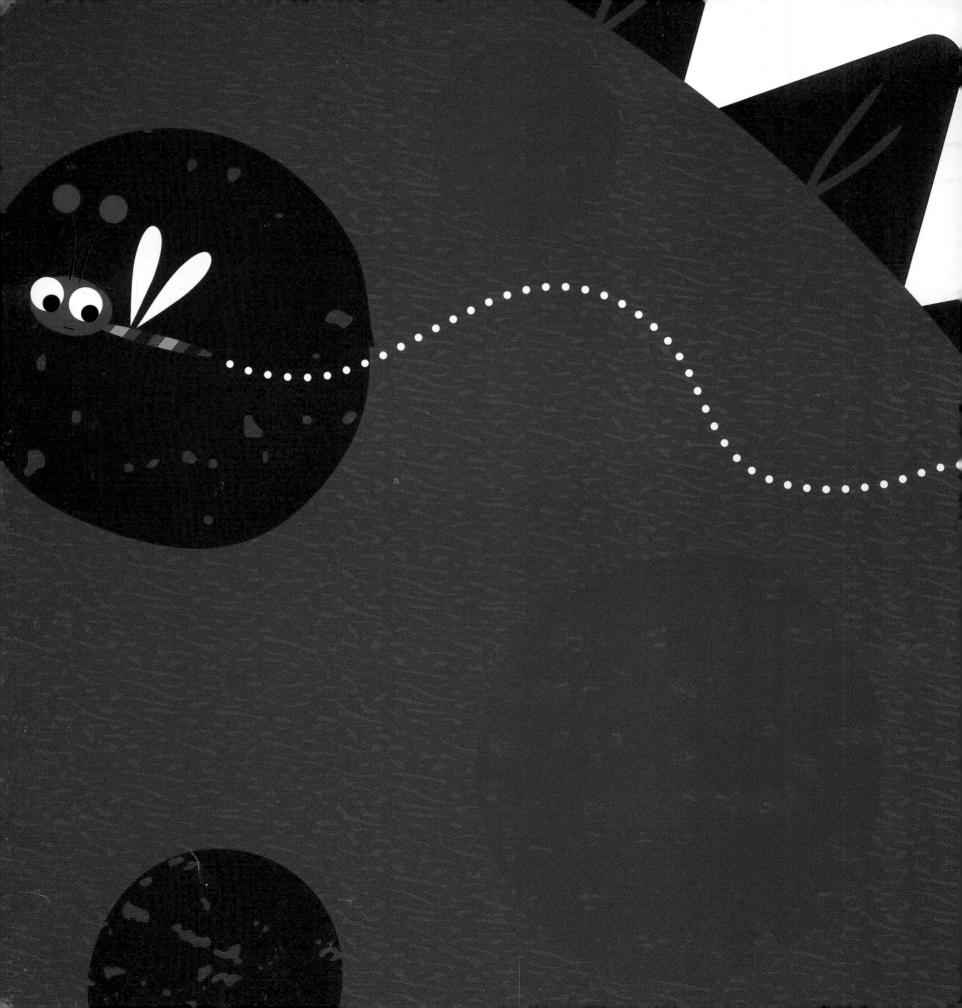

Right. EVEN YOU won't be able to . . .

. . . point to your nose,

touch your toes,

find a rose,

and shout,

"Banana!"

Have you done this before?

It's **lucky** I have a plan . . .

You must never touch a **T. rex**, unless you . . .

find a rose,

I COUNT 2 to three, 3

touch your toes,

Wave at me,

. . . point to your nose,

Shout, "BANANA!"

GLUE

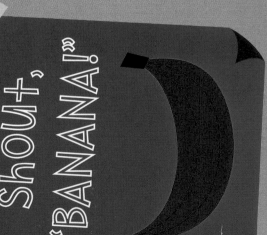

meow
like a cat,
SECURITY
FLAP
like a
BAT,
T.rex
Team
Raptor
sing HIGH,
then low,
SAAAAAAY
SOOOMETHIIIIING
SLOOOOOWWWW . . .

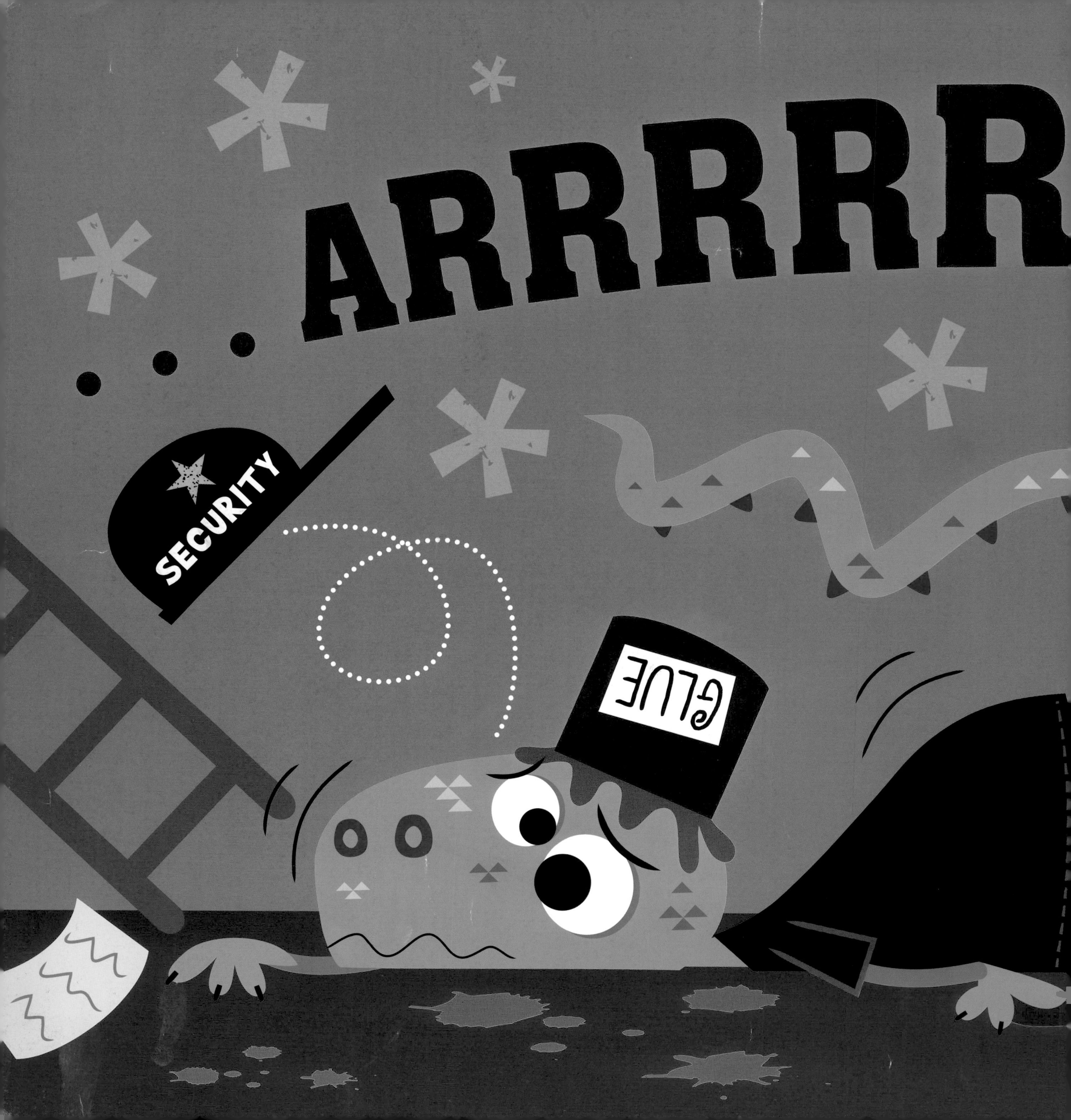
...ARRRRRR
SECURITY
GLUE

"HELLO!

Sorry about the guard.

There's really only **one** **rule** you need to know.

You must never touch a **T. rex**, unless you . . .

ASK POLITELY.

Go on, give it a try!"

"How **nice** and **polite** you are!

OF COURSE

YOU CAN!"

Okay, okay.

You're brighter than I thought.
But I've got one more rule for you:

DON'T CLOSE
this book!

THE END

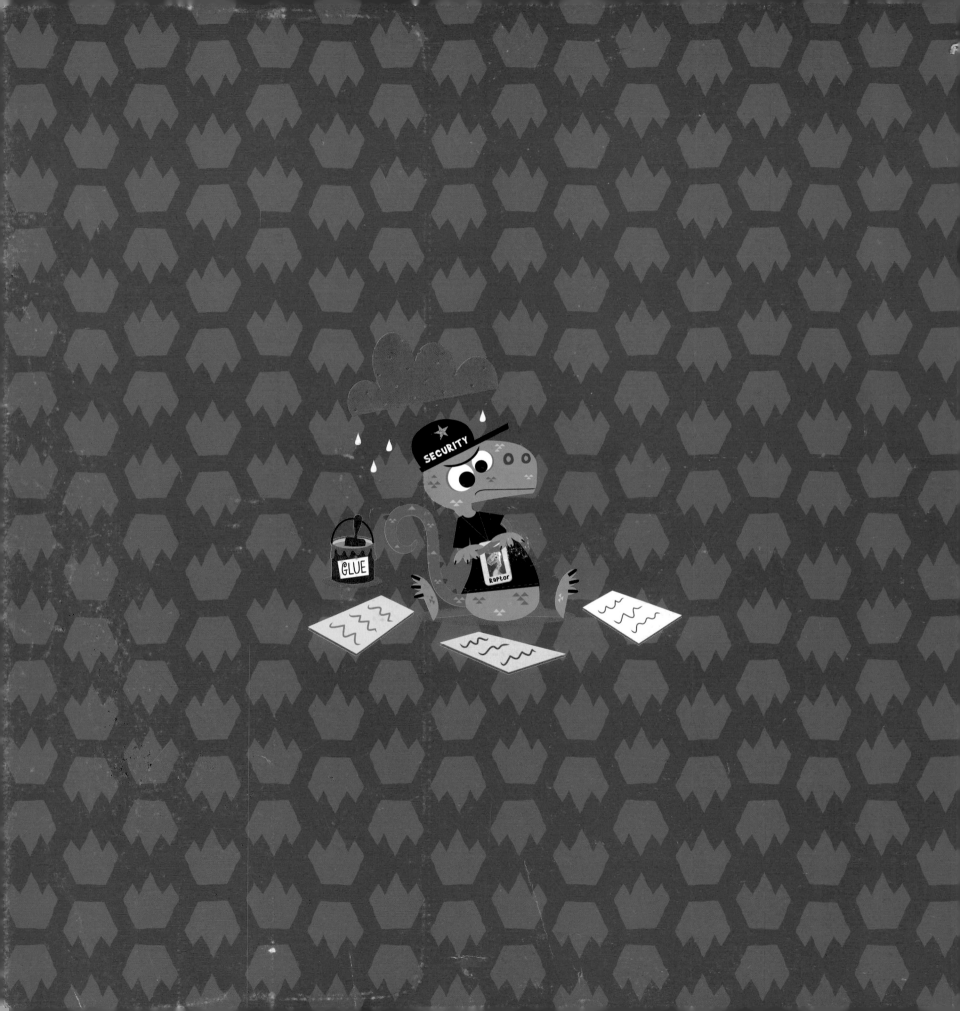